STEALING CHRISTMAS

MAGICAL MATCHMAKER, BOOK 1

AMANDA ADAMS

ABOUT: STEALING CHRISTMAS

My job is stressing me out.

My engagement is a joke.

And I can't stop thinking about a man I can't have.

Zach Stahl.

Tall, dark and handsome?

Check.

But he's dating my boss - a vicious witch I do not want to cross.

Besides, I'm nobody.

Why would he want me?

I would need a certified fairy-godmother to pull this one off.

A smoking hot, red dress.

And the courage to go after what I want.

Maybe, just maybe, I can find a way to melt Zach's Stahl's heart.

 achary Steal

EVERY OTHER DAY of the year I beg them to finish the stupid meeting already. I mean, damn, we talk about the same shit every day. It's like these tech guys must use every minute of scheduled time just so they don't have to get back to real work. And I can't stand meetings. Design and review and design and review, then do it all over again. There is no way I'd subject myself to this daily torture if I had any confidence at all that these nerds wouldn't ruin my designs.

Yeah, the tech nerds needed a real motorcycle guy and I'm their man. But not a single meeting goes by that I don't wish to be outside instead. A bad day riding is better than the best meeting.

But today the office barracuda will be waiting for me. Alexa Sinclair is our top account rep. She's good at what she does, which is sell my bikes to retailers all over the country. But she's way too complicated for me. Four-inch heels and a miniskirt in the office isn't my style. I get it. Sex sells and wavy blond hair, pouty lips and killer legs make any real man pay attention.

For the first time ever, I'd be thrilled if our daily meeting ran into lunch. I'm hoping, if we run late, Alexa will be gone already and not waiting to ambush me… again.

And I can't put her off any longer. With the Christmas party now two days away, she has become more and more persistent. She first asked me to take her to the party two weeks before Thanksgiving. Yesterday she texted me twice and sent an *oh so innocent* follow up email. Hell, for all I know, the only thing she hasn't resorted to, getting on her knees and begging, is waiting for me outside the conference room door.

"Well, here goes nothin'." I didn't mean for anybody to hear but Sam caught what I said as I exhaled the words under my breath and rose to my feet.

"What's that?" Sam asks. Sam's a good guy. Mid-twenties, electrical engineering degree from M.I.T., and smart as hell.

"Oh, nothing. Just talking to myself."

"You're usually the first one out of the meeting. You okay?"

"Yeah, I'm fine." I follow him out the door, grinning

when I spot the wild cowlick on the back of his head. Like all the other tech guys, Sam is wearing wrinkled khakis, a button up shirt and dress shoes. I don't exactly fit in with my black tee shirt, jeans and leather boots, and I don't care either.

I hope he'll continue to his desk without wanting to carry on an awkward conversation. But no such luck. He pauses and waits for me to sidle up next to him. It's not that I don't like the guy, he's cool and very genuine, I'm just not one for office small talk.

"So." He pauses as though struggling to create a topic of conversation. "Any big plans this weekend?"

"Just the Christmas party." I glance to my right to see if I can catch a glimpse of Alexa in her office but her door is closed. As I turn back to face Sam I notice Bethany, Alexa's assistant, talking on the phone but looking straight at me. When I catch her eye, she looks down and covers her face with her left hand.

She looks incredible today, like every other day, so beautiful in a natural sort of way. The best part of my day is leaving the design meeting and walking past her desk; I anticipate those five seconds every day, even if I only catch a glimpse. I love that she doesn't have to work hard to look amazing; she is one of the few girls in the office that doesn't cake on her makeup. And those glasses, I love those glasses, the hot for teacher type.

Damn, I'd like to have her horizontal, wearing nothing but those glasses. I wonder if she knows about Alexa and the Christmas party. If I thought she would say yes, I'd ask her to be my date to the party. But she would never go for someone like me. She's a good girl type, dresses like a Puritan, and she probably thinks I'm a hard-core biker jerk. Hell, she's never even spoken to me.

Sam is fidgeting, obviously uncomfortable. "How about you? Are you going?" I ask Sam.

"I doubt it, I don't have a date. How about you? I'm sure you have a date."

"No, not yet." I pat him on the shoulder as I stop and turn to head toward Bethany. "Hey Sam, I don't mean to ditch you but you reminded me I need to talk to Alexa."

He smiles and nods as the realization hits him. "Oh, I see. Good luck." He winks and laughs as he heads down the hall.

Everybody expects me to date girls like Alexa, hot, sexy, full-court press kind of girls. That's why Sam smiled. To be honest, she is attractive. She always wears sexy clothes; high heels, shorts skirts, low cut blouses and loads of jewelry. She wears a ton of makeup and her hair is always perfect to the point of being over-done. I'm sure she spends two hours getting ready for work every morning.

She looks great. She's just not my type.

And yet, I've decided to give in and throw myself upon the altar of Alexa's relentless pursuit. I don't want to go to the Christmas party alone.

As I near Bethany's desk she stands up and ends her telephone conversation. "Oh my God," she says into the receiver. "I have to go, I'll see you in a few minutes."

She smiles at me for the first time and I nearly forget why I'm there. My God, is there anything more perfect than a gorgeous woman smiling. "Hot date?" I ask.

"Mmm hmm." Her cheeks turn bright red and she looks at her desk. "Wait, no. That's just my best friend. We're having lunch together."

She grabs her stapler and a stack of papers that are already fastened together, and staples them again. "What can I… how can I… Is there something I can do for you?" Still looking down, she sits in her chair and staples the papers one more time.

"I'm Zach Steal." She looks up into my eyes but doesn't say a word. "I think you stapled both sides of the paper." As I pause and smile, she sits frozen. Am I that fucking scary? "Is Alexa in?"

"Uhhhh." She turns in her chair and crosses her legs as she looks at Alexa's office door. From what I can see of her legs, peeking out from under a long flowing skirt, they are spectacular. I follow the line of her thighs up the length of her body to her right hand that has moved up to her collarbone as her neck twists with her body. The delicate soft line of her neck leads to her distinct jaw line and flawless face. "No. She's… I'm Bethany, no… Bethany's not in, I mean she's not in, she's out, I'm in." She looks at me in the eye again, shakes her head and smiles.

"You're Bethany," I tell her. "Bethany Riley."

"Right, sorry. I knew that."

"So, Alexa's not in?" I smile at her and can't help but notice her amazing breasts beneath her cardigan sweater. This woman has more curves than a winding mountain road and I'd love to explore every turn. And she's adorable; I think she's embarrassed.

"No."

She pulls the sides of her sweater tight over her breasts as though she noticed me admiring them. I almost don't care that she caught me looking until I notice the ring on her left hand. Damn, shit and damn, the hottest girl in the office is married? Of course, she's married, she's the hottest girl in the office.

Now I regret checking her out, so I ask. "Are you and your husband going to the Christmas party?" My attempt at covering my idiocy with conversation appears lame, even to me, but she doesn't seem to notice.

"Yes. What? No." She pauses and stands up with a frustrated look on her face. "I mean, yes I am going to the party but no, he's not my, I'm not married."

Why does that news make me so damn happy? So, she's engaged. That's still not something I will move on, no matter how hot she is. I don't play that game. "Well, I'm sure I'll see you there. Can you tell Alexa I stopped by?"

She plops back into her chair, slumps against the backrest and says, "Sure".

Before either of us embarrasses ourselves any further, I smile and walk toward the shop. As I walk away, I turn and call out, "Nice to finally meet you, Bethany."

She has her face covered in her hands and is shaking her head. Without looking up she raises one hand and waves in my direction.

What the heck was that all about? She seemed really out of sorts and I have no idea why. But I liked it.

ethany Riley

As I STAND in front of the double silver doors waiting for the elevator to arrive I glance at my phone to check the time. Lindsey will be so mad at me for arriving late but, given the circumstances, she will forgive me today. I contemplate texting her, to tell her I am on my way, but the elevator arrives and I enter the metal box of doom.

As the door closes I am encased in an envelope of sweat and perfume. To complete my personal version of hell, the elevator echoes with the straining, techno notes of a terrible instrumental version of a recent pop hit.

Why do they butcher the music? Why not just play the real songs?

Unfortunately, I recognize the music and recall all

the words. The lyrics run inside my head, telling me how I missed out on love.

"Shut up, Taylor," I think to myself, but the song plays on.

Okay, all right, so my first conversation with the hottest guy on the face of the planet could have gone worse. To top off the whole horrible, embarrassing, soul-crushing incident, I could have thrown up on myself.

There's always next time.

Hah! Zach Steal will never talk to me again, I'm sure of it.

As the elevator arrives at the lobby, I wade into a mass of bodies heading out to lunch, and my only thought remains with him. Zach Steal. Damn, he is hot and so handsome and… so damn hot. And he finally talked to me.

He is not the type of guy that a girl like me is supposed to go for. He's huge, and a biker, and covered in tattoos, and oh to see more of those tattoos. I imagine he smells of motor oil and sweat, but I would love to get up close and find out for myself.

As I head down the sidewalk toward the Get Perky coffee shop, and my date with Lindsey, I can't help but imagine what he might do to me if we were to shower together. I'd definitely help him wash off the effects of a hard day's work in the shop. Something tells me a guy like that would do things to me I never imagined could be done.

As we stand in the shower together, facing each other, he

kisses me, as though it is the last kiss we will ever share. The press of his muscular frame holds me in place and his huge cock presses against my belly. He pulls back and stares into my eyes with the expression of a determined man full of hunger. His large hands move to my shoulders and spin me in place. He presses against my back and I feel every inch of him as his arms wrap around me and he nuzzles my neck with his lips.

"Don't move" he whispers in my ear.

He moves away, reaches for the soap and I wait in antici-pation as he builds lather in his hands. I sense his eyes studying my body from behind and I wait as he turns the soap in his hands. My God, please hurry, *I think to myself.*

And then he begins. He starts at my neck and I tilt my head back into his strong fingers to expose more of my skin to his touch. His hands glide across my skin and he covers my body with the scent of sunflower and honey. As he moves to my shoulders, he tightens his grip and gently massages my muscles to release the tension of my day. I drop my head and stretch my neck as all my stress leaves my body. He builds more lather and moves down my back to my round bottom.

His hands move in and around every curve and crevasse, I shudder as he nears all my sensitive areas and I want to beg him to linger longer and move deeper. But he is an expert and builds my desire, leaving to move down my thighs as I rock against his strong grip. He moves up and down the length of each leg with just the right amount of pressure, massaging each calf before moving back to the top of each thigh.

As he reaches the top of my left thigh he brushes against my swollen folds and I moan with pleasure. He's teasing me, I can tell, because he pulls away, moves to my right thigh and begins again. This time I groan before he even reaches my sensitive area, and he doesn't disappoint, pressing harder this time yet he moves away, too quickly again. I love it.

He stands and presses against me as he reaches around to my breasts. My nipples ache in their reach for his touch. He glides over and around massaging my heavy breasts. I lean back into him and tilt my head into his shoulder. Is he going to make me beg? His touch is purposeful and torturous as he leaves my erect nipples aching for his attention.

He slides the length of his cock between the mounds of my soapy bottom and presses harder against me. My breath catches in my throat as I glide up and down his length and lean forward, praying he will take me now, fuck me now.

"Uh-uh. Not yet." He pulls me upright, grabs the showerhead and rinses me clean. As he spins me back toward him to rinse my front, he is grinning as though he senses my anticipation and loves making me wait.

After we exit the shower he stands before me and dries himself while I wait, his message has been clear. I am his to command and right now I am to wait and watch. His entire tattooed body ripples with muscles as he completes the task, the lines of his shoulders and arms stretch and flex as he moves across his entire body with his towel. He smiles into my eyes as he dries his cock; I see the anticipation in his eyes as he prepares to bend me to his will.

He grabs a fresh towel and moves to my side. He studies each curve of my body with his eyes as he dries every inch. I shiver at his touch but I am not cold.

After finishing he tosses the towel aside, looks me in the eye and grabs my hand. "Now... come with me." I nod, speechless, onboard with whatever he wants to do next.

We enter his bedroom and I head toward his massive king size bed. "No, not yet." His deep voice commands as he steers me toward a large armchair at the foot of the bed. He pulls me in front of him and presses up against me, warm against my cool back. "Are you ready for me?"

I can only nod.

A towel covers one side of the chair and I notice a wire running from under the fabric as he bends me over the padded arm of the chair. My bottom spreads, stretched and open to the air, and to his eyes. I am instantly wet. He reaches beneath the towel, adjusts the lump and my clit settles over the bulge. He groans, touches my rounded bottom, and massages my ass and upper thighs. I drip with anticipation as his fingers near. He wets a finger by sliding it along my folds and I want to beg him to enter me. But I can't, I shouldn't.

"Please", I say.

I ache with desire and close my eyes to focus on his hand as he thrusts a finger into me. In and out he moves, slow at first then faster. I am stretched wider as he adds another large finger and moan with pleasure while he thrusts faster and faster.

My mind swirls in ecstasy and I near nirvana when he swats my left cheek with the palm of his hand. I've never been spanked before and I am shocked that I love it. "Not so fast," he commands and I pant with pleasure.

He places the large head of his cock at my wet opening and presses against me. I try to move against him, to hurry him, but he smacks my ass again. "No, no, no," he says. "You wait for me." And I am wild. My head spins with pleasure.

"Please." I say again.

"You've only begun to beg."

He thrusts his huge cock deep inside and pauses, full and deep, the entire length of him presses into me. I try to move, desperate for him to continue, and he reddens my ass again. Smack. "I said, you wait for me."

"Please", I beg.

He moves, slow at first and then faster and my pleasure builds. Reaching across my body to my shoulders, he runs his fingers up and down my back as he thrusts again and again, harder each time. "Are you ready", he asks. All I can do is moan in response.

One hand leaves my back as he continues his thrusts. He flips a switch and my entire body is shocked alive by a vibration at my clit. Hidden beneath the towel is a vibrator. I scream with desire and he thrusts with abandon as I am rocked to my core and he smacks my ass again sending me into my bliss, he joins me and groans with pleasure while he fills me with his seed…

Honk! Honk!

I stop my walk just in time to avoid a speeding sedan. The red hand of the crosswalk light reminds me I have not been paying attention during my walk to the coffee shop and yet here I am, arrived already. I can see Lindsey staring at me through the window and waiting for me at a table. She shrugs at me and shakes her head. All I can do is smile and fan myself. How can I be so hot? It's December and can't be over 40 degrees out. The light changes and I head into my favorite coffee shop to deal with Lindsey's curious gaze.

"Where have you been? You're late."

3

LINDSEY'S SCOLDING ME AGAIN, acting like a big sister more than a friend. She pulls the sister act when she thinks I am messing up.

"I've had quite a day."

"What is going on? Come on, spill it. You're flushed." She ducks lower and whispers, "If I didn't know better, I would say you just finished having sex."

I glance around and over my shoulder to make sure nobody can hear. The only person within earshot is an elderly lady seated behind me, but she is probably hard of hearing anyway. "He finally talked to me."

"Who, the hot guy at work? Is that why you hung up on me?"

"Yep."

"You bitch. Tell me everything." Lindsey leans forward in her chair.

"Did you order us anything?" I ask and turn toward the front counter as I realize we have nothing to drink.

"Yes, now stop delaying and tell me."

"Ugggh." I lean back in my chair and laugh at my pitiful self. "I made an ass of myself, couldn't even remember my own name. How could I be such an idiot? There is no way he will ever want to talk to me again."

"Well, what did he say?"

"I was so flustered, I can't even remember." I shrug my shoulders and sit up in my chair. "It doesn't matter. He only stopped to talk to Alexa, anyway."

"You are so much prettier than her."

"Thanks, but she seems more his type. He probably likes the slutty type. There is a reason she gets so much attention at work."

"Because she acts like a prostitute." Lindsey rolls her eyes. "Trust me, a real man doesn't want that, not long term. That's the kind of girl you screw, but you don't, what?"

"Take home to meet your mother." I finish Lindsey's sentence.

"Exactly."

I've heard her preach it a thousand times. Trouble is, women like Alexa always seem to have dates. Meanwhile, up-tight good girls like us? We sit home every Valentine's day watching bad movies and eating chocolate ice cream. Even last year. My fiancé got roped into working on a big corporate client's tax documents. Engaged, at last, and still alone for every major holiday.

I need to invest in some make-up and heels.

No. I'd just end up looking like a clown and falling on my ass.

"Well he didn't stop just to talk to me." I place my elbows on the table and rest my chin in my hands. "At least he asked if I was going to the Christmas party. That is more than enough for me today."

"Wait. What do you mean? Did you? Were you daydreaming again? Is that why you were so flushed and nearly got run over?"

I only needed to smile in response and Lindsey burst out laughing.

"You are so bad."

A young guy behind the counter called out, "Two vanilla lattes for Lindsey."

"Pause," Lindsey said as she stood and moved toward the counter. "You're telling me everything and don't even think about skipping any details."

By the time we finish our first round of lattes, and I finish my story, Lindsey could only say, "Oh my God, oh my God, you are so bad. So bad." She pauses and stares into space. "So bad." She checks her phone. "And now I have to go."

"What?" I said. "So soon? We haven't even had our second round."

"You were late, bitch." I've never understood why

she loves calling me that, but I take it as a sign of affection. "I have to go back to work. Michael is in the office today and I never miss any time when he is in, if you know what I mean."

"Who's bad now?" She's always had a crush on her boss even though he is at least ten years older than her. It didn't hurt that he made over a billion dollars when he sold his first tech company to one of the big three. Handsome. Smart. Rich. Yeah, she has it bad for him.

"A girl can dream." She leans over and hugs me. "I paid for a pastry for you, just pick one out."

"You mean you flirted with the kid behind the counter and he offered you one for free?"

"At least I've still got it." She smiles and waves as she walks out the door.

I walk to the counter and wait as the young guy behind the counter finishes with a customer. His nametag is a generic, *Hi, My Name is:*. The name *Chris* is written in barely legible black marker beneath the label. He looks about my age with long blond hair, blue eyes, a nice smile and a wanna-be beard that is more like an overgrown goat in need of a trim. I cast him my best flirting smile and wave him over. "Hey Chris, my friend said I could pick out a pastry?"

"Sure." He smiles at me and pauses a little too long, his gaze a little too direct. "She said you thought I was hot."

"Oh, she did, did she?" Damn Lindsey, she is always pulling shit like this. I lie and say, "Well, you are very cute. And she shouldn't be telling all my secrets."

That last bit makes his eyes light up.

"Can I have a piece of pumpkin bread?"

He wraps up a huge piece of warm bread and hands it to me. "You wanna go out sometime?"

"Oh, sorry." I say and wave my left hand in the air. "I'm engaged."

"You're savage." He wags his finger at me as I walk back to my table. "I'm going to keep my eye on you two."

As I sit down at the table to enjoy my "gift" from Lindsey, I smile and shake my head. Lindsey. That little turkey is always trying to jam me up like that, with all kinds of men. My phone vibrates, and it's a text from her, it's almost as though she can sense that I am laughing at her. A simple smiley face with its tongue sticking out says it all. Now it's my turn to call her a bitch. I type it in my phone with my free hand, press send and smile again as a hand touches my shoulder.

The little old lady that was seated behind me moves up beside me. Before I can react, she's joined me, a kind smile on her face. "Hello Dearie", she says in the sweetest old lady voice.

"Oh, hello."

"I don't mean to intrude." She reaches down and grabs hold of my hand. "I couldn't help but overhear your story. The one you told your girlfriend."

"Oh my God. No." I sense my face turn red with heat. "I'm sorry. I shouldn't be talking so loud."

"I thought it was wonderful, you made it all sound so wonderful."

"I am so embarrassed." I swallow hard on the bite of pumpkin bread I didn't realized I still held in my mouth. "You didn't hear everything, did you?"

"Oh, yes." She nods "I just love hearing stories of true love."

"Oh, no." I shake my head. "We're not really in love. I barely know him and I'm not really his type." Besides, I'm engaged.

"I think you might surprise yourself, if you try. True love is often found where you least expect it. Trust me, sometimes an old lady knows more than you think." Her eyes twinkle, I can't decide if they're green or blue, and her smile grows wider as I am captivated by her stare. Her lips are painted a bright, cheerful red. And her cheekbones, when she smiles, you could trace them with a pencil.

"Yes, but, but…"

"Yes, I know." She interrupts. "But you're not really engaged, you just need to tell him. It's not going to work out. And don't worry, dear. He knows."

"How do you know that?" Now I am freaking out. How could she know about my boring, work-a-holic fiancé and our less than passionate sex life?

"I told you. Sometimes an old lady just knows these things." She rubs the top of my hand and a tingle runs up my arm and into my chest. My head spins and I grab the table with my free hand to keep from falling out of my chair. The room is spinning, full tilt-a-whirl, just got off the carnival ride, spin. "Just trust in your heart.

Everything you need lies within in you. Your true love, and your destiny, awaits." She pats my hand and turns to walk away.

I am speechless as the door closes behind her. I breathe deep and hold onto the table until the spinning stops. I sit in silence with my mouth hanging open. Am I more embarrassed or stunned? The poor old lady overheard my tale of raunchy shower sex… but seemed to like it.

Okay… a little weird and humiliating but… okay. But how could she know about Elliott? Our relationship died a slow and uneventful death months ago. And true, we hadn't talked about it yet, but we both understood. I just hadn't seen him to give him his grandmother's ring back.

Our parents will cry when we tell them. We've been together for three years. But I'm not about to marry a man just to make our mothers happy.

Elliott's a decent enough guy, but milquetoast boring and more interested in his work than me. And he's an accountant, a man who actually *enjoys* working the numbers.

I want a man who enjoys working me.

We acted the part after announcing our engagement, the whole debacle arranged by our parents, but passion never joined our play. We both came to realize that we have nothing in common and less than zero chemistry in the bedroom. I want a man to take charge in bed and crave my body like a caveman. Trouble is, I think Elliott wants the same thing. He always wanted to be bossed around in bed. I mean, not by a guy... at least I don't think so.

I get it, some guys like that from a woman, but I want a man with raw animal lust for my body, an out-of-control craving he unleashes at just the right moment. I want someone like the Zach of my dreams.

And the little old woman was right. Elliott and I are over.

I noticed Zach glance at my hand. If I hadn't been wearing this ring, he might have asked me to the Christmas party.

Hah! A girl can dream.

Right then I decide to call Elliott on my way back to the office. I need to give him back his ring. Time to make it official.

I didn't plan on doing anything this weekend. And, a few hours ago, I had no intention of going to the Christmas party. But all that tingling must have made me crazy. I'm feeling powerful and strong. I'm one hundred percent sure what I want and it's time to take charge of my life.

I want Zach Steal. Under me. Over me. Inside me.

I want caveman sex.

First, I'll need a sexy red dress.

I pull out my phone and text Lindsey before I get up to return to work. I'll need her help. I'm uncertain what that old lady did but my body is humming like I'm made of electricity. My fingers fly across my screen as I type.

It's caveman hunting season... Send.

And I have a Christmas party to go to. Devil smiley face. Send.

4

As I STAND on the sidewalk waiting for the car to pick me up, I dig my finger under the stiff collar of my starched white shirt and pull it away from my neck. I can't stand ties and stiff dress shirts. In fact, I have spent my entire life avoiding situations that necessitate wearing formal clothing. But I get it. It's Christmas and everybody wants a Christmas party.

Not me, but everybody else.

I'm only going because the partners insisted I come and bring a date.

Alexa screamed in the phone when I called her to accept her invitation. And she insisted that we arrive in style. Which is why I'm standing in the freezing cold waiting for the damn limousine. If I had driven, we would be there already.

Where is this fucking guy?

I'm about ready to get in my truck when a set of headlights turns the corner and the black car pulls to the curb in front of me. The driver hops out and hurries around the car to open the back door.

"Thanks, you didn't have to do that, I can get the door myself." I've never liked making a workingman work harder than they already do. Not on my account.

"My pleasure, sir." He opens the door and motions for me to enter.

As I duck to enter the back seat, two long legs greet me and I follow them up to a tight blue dress and Alexa's smiling face. She shifts her hips left, turns her knees my direction and crosses her legs. Wow. This woman is a pro, and she is not afraid to put all her assets on display. She has amazing legs, and that dress leaves little to the imagination. I smile and sit next to her. "Hey, Alexa."

"Hi, Zach."

"I thought I was being picked up first."

"Well, I wanted to have maximum time in the car with you, before the party." She smiles and reaches for a glass half full of what looks like straight Scotch, no ice. "Would you like a drink?"

"No, I'm fine."

"You sure?" She reaches down and puts her hand on my knee. "It might help warm you up."

Typical Alexa. She comes out with both barrels blazing. If I wanted, we could skip the party, go up to my place and get down to business right now. Hell, I'm shocked she hasn't suggested it already.

But she likes to show off and make her presence felt, hence the limousine and the incredible dress. I'm not so sure I'm not just part of her show for the night. Alexa turns to the window and sips her drink with perfectly painted lips.

"I stopped by your office the other day."

"You did?"

"Didn't Bethany tell you?"

"Who?"

"Bethany." I can't tell Alexa but I want to say, *you know, the girl I haven't been able to stop thinking about.* "She sits right outside your office. She's young and blonde, wears glasses."

She turns back to face me with intense interest, almost alarm on her face and I wish I hadn't brought it up. "Oh, that girl."

"Bethany works for you, right?"

"She helps several account reps, but yes she works for me, though I rarely talk to her."

"She seems very nice."

"Oh, Zach." Alexa smiles and moves her hand up to my thigh. "Naughty girls are so much more fun. And we are going to have a lot of fun tonight."

When we arrive at the party Alexa moves into full socialite mode. I've never heard more phony, small talk in my life. She's an expert. She must have a master's degree in bullshit with a doctorate in ego stroking. I'm sure every financial partner over the age of fifty has a hard on by the time she's done stroking their backs and their egos. After the first hour, I'm about ready to throw up and I'm exhausted. I can't wait to go home, to escape; yet I haven't spoken a word.

Alexa doesn't let go of me until we cover every social circle, spending extra time with the executives, and everybody knows we've arrived, and that we are *together*. When we reach the CEO's table, she finally releases my arm and sits down. "Zach, honey, will you please get us a drink? You know what I like." She shoots me her fake smile before turning her attention to Jack Simpson, the CEO.

I know Jack and he knows me. We share a discreet smile as I roll my eyes and head to the bar. I have no idea what this woman drinks and I don't care either.

Thankfully, the bar is on the other side of the room and I take my sweet time getting there.

I nod to the bartender. "How you doin' tonight?"

"Good, sir. How are you?"

I pull a twenty-dollar bill out of my wallet and put it in his tip jar. "It'll be great if you don't call me sir." I reach up to my tight as fuck shirt collar and unbutton the top two buttons so I can breathe. "My name is Zach. What's yours?"

"Thank you, brother." He reaches across the bar and shakes my hand. I see he's got ink from wrist to elbow and I grin. My kind of guy. "I'm Joe. What can I get you?"

"Joe, I need two drinks. I'll take a Jack and Coke.

And the second drink, I don't give a fuck. Just make me something for a woman."

"Coming right up."

I turn back to the party to watch the sea of humanity as I wait. The dance floor is empty. Though the DJ is pumping out electronica, not enough drinks are flowing to embolden everyone to flail about and feel the beat. Most of the employees are milling around tables getting acquainted, feeling each other out in the party setting. I only recognize about ten percent of the people, but those that I have talked to at work seem nice. Jack deserves a lot of credit, he put together a very sharp group of young techies and proud nerds.

The bartender hands me my drinks and I turn to head back to Jack's table when I see her. The most gorgeous and curvaceous woman just walked in the main entrance across the room. She looks as though every light in the place is reflecting off her pale skin and long blonde hair. Her whole body is fucking sparkling, like she's got glitter everywhere, even in her hair. And that dress. I'm getting hard for the first time tonight just looking at her body rocking that fucking dress. It's sexy, and red and damn. Her shoes are bright red and her legs a mile long.

It's Bethany.

And she is staring straight at me.

My heart seizes in my chest. I'm frozen in place and I can't breathe.

"Is this one mine?" Alexa appears out of nowhere

and blocks my view. "Thank you, sweetie. Shall we head back? I got us a place at Jack's table."

"Uh." I still haven't gained my composure and step to Alexa's side to see past her. Bethany is gone. Where could she have gone?

"Zach?" Alexa puts her arm through mine and tugs. "Shall we?"

5

Bethany

As I STAND in front of the mirror one last time I almost can't believe my eyes. My dress is amazing. So what if my outfit cost me a whole paycheck? I don't care.

But what if Zach doesn't want me? What if he decides not to show up after all? I doubt a fancy Christmas party is his kind of thing. "You sure I look okay? Not too slutty?" I ask Lindsey.

"You are a spectacular vision. If he has a penis, he won't be able to resist. Hell, I don't have one and I almost can't resist. Your ass looks positively sizzling. If you don't leave soon, you could be in trouble."

"You're so ridiculous."

"I am so aware of that, so go. You're going to be late already. You're beautiful and smart and beautiful and nice and smoking hot and beautiful. Trust me, he's doomed and doesn't even know it yet."

"Thank you so much for coming over to help me get ready."

"You're my girl. We'd do anything for each other." Lindsey grabs my glasses off my dresser and hands them to me. "Here, you won't be able to find him without these." She holds up my black glasses and crinkles her nose as she inspects them. "You're sure this is the all you have? They don't match the ensemble. They should be red."

"My other pair broke, this is all I have."

"Well, I guess black goes with anything. They'll do." She puts them on my face and smiles as she grabs my shoulders and turns me toward the door. "Now, go get him." She smacks me on the ass like a football player. "Yum."

"You're so crazy. I love you."

"Love you back. Good luck."

Lindsey ordered me a car, and the driver arrives just as I walk out the front door. What would I do without her? I wish she could go with me; she is always the life of the party, smart, funny, bold and loves to flirt. I'm not one for small talk, but when she is with me, I never worry. She does all the talking for me. I begged and begged her to go. Not tonight, she insisted. For some stupid reason, she thinks tonight I need to be on my own. And she is right. I can do this. I must do this.

I take a deep breath as the car arrives at the hotel. A hotel valet opens the door for me and I tip the driver as

I step into the cool night air. Unable to move, I stand and stare at the hotel entrance, doubts creep into my mind.

This is all just a huge mistake. What I was thinking? I realize just how cold it is. All the money I spent on this outfit and I forgot a sweater to cover my bare shoulders. I should go back to my apartment to get one. Maybe I should go back to my apartment and forget this whole thing.

I turn around to get back in the car but it's too late. The car is gone. Damn, I guess I have to go in after all.

I head down red-carpeted hallway after red-carpeted hallway searching for the darn ballroom. Why don't they mark these things better? Then I recognize several people from the office who seem confident with the direction they are headed so I follow them.

They stop at the coat-check room beside the ballroom and I head through the main entrance and stop. What now? Find someone I recognize? Find a corner to hide in?

I glance across the dance floor and spot the bar. That's a good place to start; liquid courage is bound to help. And there he is. Zach Steal. And he is staring right at me. My heart jumps in my chest and I freeze. Why is he staring? Is there something wrong with my outfit? Is my dress too short?

My God, he looks great. I start to smile and someone blocks my view. Blue dress. Hot body. Heels an inch higher than the ones I'm teetering in.

Shit.

Alexa.

Why is she talking to him? I am totally freaking out. Please tell me I'm not seeing what I think I'm seeing.

He can't be here with her. Fate wouldn't be that cruel.

Is that why he stopped by my desk looking for her? Is that his date?

I turn and walk in the opposite direction as fast as I can in these damn high heels.

Zach

I'M desperate as I search the room while Alexa drags me beside her. Bethany is gone, nowhere in sight. Did I imagine her? Am I losing my mind? How could she have disappeared so fast?

Dinner at Jack's table seems to drag on forever but for his continual grinning at me. He can tell I'm miserable. He knows, and he's laughing at me. I can see it in his eyes. The situation is kind of funny. Alexa never stops talking, never stops cackling, all too amused by everything Jack says. I almost burst out laughing several times as he rolls his eyes in my direction. If she only knew Jack well enough to know his low tolerance for social climbing kiss-asses, she would dial it back.

I'm too distracted to stop Alexa from embarrassing herself. I scan the room non-stop, trying to find Bethany, yet I can't. Did she leave already? Did I imagine the whole thing?

"Zach, honey." Alexa tugs on my sleeve.

"What?"

"I said, aren't you excited for the launch of the new model next week? The design team really outdid themselves with this one."

"Huh? Oh yeah, sure." Our new bike has all the geeky bells and whistles, but looks like a hard-core rider's dream. She's fast, sleek, and can give any street bike on the market a run for the money. But Alexa is looking at me with the glassy-eyed, false smile she uses when she's making a sale. She has no idea I designed the bike from the ground up. Hell, she has no idea I own a large part of the company.

She wants to fuck a bad boy. Trouble is, I'm not interested in what she's offering.

"Excuse me. I'm going to the restroom." I say as I stand up and excuse myself from the table.

"Okay, but don't be gone long. You owe me a dance."

As I walk around the outside of the ballroom, I search every table and dark corner. If I see that red dress, it will catch my eye in an instant. But Bethany is nowhere, disappeared like smoke in the wind.

I head out to the lobby to escape the frenzied atmosphere of the party and search for a comfortable place to sit. A solitary large grey chair that looks out over the city through a set of large, plate glass windows draws me in and I sink into its cushions. The clock on the tower outside shows 9:30. If I sit here long enough, I will have exhausted enough time at the party so I can make my excuses and leave. I doubt Alexa noticed I haven't returned. She's busy with Jack and is in full schmoozing mode.

As I sit and relax, my mind can only think of going to work on Monday. Bethany will be back at her desk, watching me as I leave the design meeting and I won't let her disappear on me again. My mind races with thoughts of what I might say.

The sound of laughter from the front desk snaps me out of my trance and I glance down at my watch to see that twenty minutes have passed as I daydreamed. Alexa hasn't bothered to come find me. I am relieved but I should head back into the fray, make one final appearance so I can leave.

I walk across the lobby and head down the hallway toward the ballroom wondering what excuse I can come up with to leave. As I turn the corner and cross into a wall of sound and flashing lights, I spot the red dress walking along the edge of the dance floor toward the bar.

I didn't imagine her or that dress. She is here and I've never seen anything look so good.

The fabric accentuates every curve of her body. An

open back exposes the pale skin of her spine down to her curvy ass. Every step reinvents sex in motion, under sparkling red cover, and I have to get my hands on her. I could spend an entire afternoon on that ass in that dress. I pick up my pace to catch her and reach out when I get close enough. My palm grasps the top of her hand, just as she reaches the far edge of the dance floor.

"Dance with me." My palm on her hand feels like I'm touching fire. An electrical jolt runs up my arm to my chest. She turns and her face lights up my night with a smile.

6

Bethany

AN HOUR in the bathroom is all it took. An hour, that's all. Now I'm fine. It took everything inside me to keep from crying my eyes out and ruining my makeup. I spent all my savings on this dress, came to this stupid Christmas party, and now what? I'm by myself and that bitch is with him, that horrible awful woman.

Okay. Fine. He can have her. If that is what he wants, what he likes, then he deserves her. No, they deserve each other.

That's what I get for lusting after a guy like that anyway. He's edgy and dark and barely talks. Tall, dark and handsome. Brooding. The typical bad boy mothers around the world plot to warn their daughters about.

What the hell was I thinking? He is way out of my

league. What would I even do with a guy like that? Make him hot cocoa and cuddle on the couch watching chick-flicks on a Friday night?

Had I imagined him grinning at me, telling me I was adorable and wiping the movie-inspired tears from my cheeks with his big, meaty hands before he fucked my brains out on the living room floor? Okay. Yeah. I'd imagined that whole scenario a few too many times. Of course I had, I'm very creative.

It's time to tell my over-active imagination to knock it off.

Maybe I should just go back to milquetoast Elliott. Sure, he'd taken the ring back and hadn't argued with me. What if even boring, steady Elliott wouldn't take me back?

Now I really want to cry.

I wander my way back through the red-carpeted halls toward the beat of the music. I'm going back into the stupid party to have at least one drink before I leave. As I stand in the doorway, I pause to search the entire room. Thank goodness, I don't see him. Maybe he's gone. The dance floor is packed and everybody else seems to be having a good time. I head for the bar. I'll be needing a straight tequila shot, or two, maybe three.

As I near the bar and move toward the queue someone grabs my hand. I turn as my arm tingles, alive with energy for the second time today. I see a large, masculine hand. Sexy. That hand is attached to an arm in a black dinner jacket. I follow the line of his arm up to those eyes. Blue as ice and smiling at me.

He asks me something, I don't hear what, nor do I care, but I nod and follow him to the dance floor. My entire body is tingling and before I realize what is happening, I am in his arms moving to music I don't even hear.

"Where did you go? I've been looking for you." Zach stares into my eyes and grins.

"You have?" I want to smack myself. The hottest man on the planet tells me he's been looking for me, and that's all I've got? Sheesh. I should have practiced talking today.

"Yes, where did you disappear to?"

I lie, "Oh, I just stepped out for a minute."

"You look exquisite. I saw you come in earlier but then you disappeared." He lowers his head to mine and his lips graze my cheek. "I've been searching for you all night."

Distracted, my gaze traces the line of tattoos just visible above his collar on the right side of his neck. I would love to find out where they end. As he pulls me closer, pressing his body against mine, I look up to find him staring into my eyes. He said something, right? Something that requires a response... "You, you look beautiful, too. I mean handsome." I stammer. He's a god among mortals. Sexy.

"Why is it I find you so adorable?"

"You do?" Wait... that didn't even make sense. Did it? Why is it that just being around him turns me into a bumbling idiot? I'm not this stupid. But whenever he's around, I regress to two-year-old, single-word sentence stupidity.

"Yes, I do. Do you have any idea how much I look forward to walking past your desk every day?"

"Me, too." He smiles down at me and pulls my hips into his. He's hard and hot and I am trying to figure out what is happening here. "I mean, I look forward to you walking past my desk every day."

"But you've never said a word to me."

"I've been too afraid. You don't seem like the kind of guy that would be interested in a girl like me." His cock stiffens against my belly and he knows I can feel it as he presses harder against me.

"You're exactly the kind of girl a guy like me would be interested in."

I pause to absorb what he said, what I'm feeling. I'm having one of those moments, the kind girls dream of, and I can't contain my excitement. *Screw it*, I say to myself, I didn't get all dolled up for nothing and I blurt out. "I've dreamt of you." My cheeks flush at my confession and I turn away for a moment, too shocked by my own admission to hold his gaze.

Heat is emanating off his body in waves or is it just me?

And I turn back to gaze into his eyes and confess all. "You might not believe me but I've thought about you since the first day you walked by my desk. And I've never done anything like this, but I knew I could tonight. I had to. I came here, in this dress, for you, tonight. Just for you."

A tap on my shoulder breaks my concentration and I turn to find Alexa behind me, staring me down.

"Bethany." She smiles in her wicked way. "I see you met my date. Zach, you know Bethany, right? She works for me, remember? Thanks for keeping him company while I freshened up, honey. You don't mind if I cut in."

"You two are here together?" I ask and turn to Zach. His smile is gone and I see the truth in his eyes, the guilt, and my heart breaks a little.

"Of course, we're here together." Alexa practically shoves at my shoulder, but Zach hasn't released his hold. "The dear even picked me up in a limousine. We've planned this date for a month and it's been divine." Alexa shoves herself between us. "Zach honey, just one more dance and we can head back to my place."

I stand, stunned into silence, and she pulls Zach away into the flow of bodies on the dance floor.

Before the tears can stream down my cheeks, I turn and walk straight out the door.

7

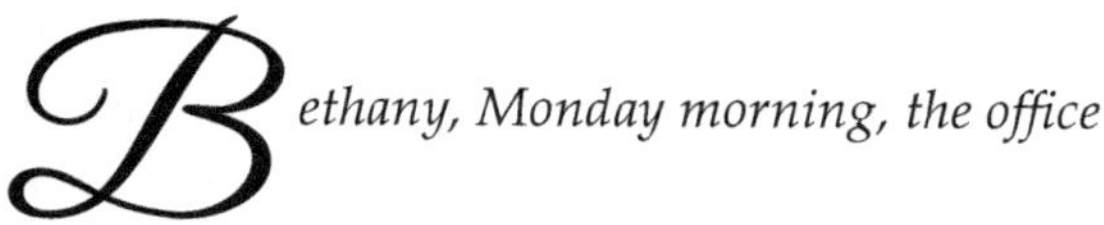
ethany, Monday morning, the office

IT'S Monday and I'm back in the elevator listening to awful canned music again. The elevator lurches beneath my feet, shooting me up through space and I dread the opening of the doors. At least I only have to work three days this week. The office closes down on Christmas Eve, which is Thursday, and I can't wait.

I tried to rally after humiliating myself at the dance, but the rest of my weekend saw little improvement. I sat around my apartment, sulking like a fool, and watched one cheesy Christmas movie after another.

When I ran out of that party like a freak, I didn't turn back. I'd never been so grateful for a filthy taxi in my life. I jumped in that car like the devil himself was chasing me. I'm sure the driver had been waiting for someone else, but I didn't care. I begged him to take me, to speed my escape and deliver me home.

The tears must have done the trick. I tried not to cry until I got home, but water kept leaking down my face. I must have seemed pathetic enough for the driver to have sympathy for me because he pulled away from that curb like we were in a spy thriller, squealing the tires like a boss. The poor guy put up with my sobbing the whole way and must have felt bad for me because he didn't even charge for the ride.

All weekend, the inevitability of Monday morning haunted my dreams, both waking and sleeping.

But honestly, was it really that bad? So what? I dumped my fiancé. So what if I confessed to the hottest guy in the office that I've been crushing on him forever? I naïvely told the office bad boy, the leather wearing, brooding, mysterious Zach Steal, that I went to the Christmas party, by myself, just for him. Worse, I admitted wearing that expensive dress, for him, too. All for him.

Oh, and I was grinding on his crotch in happy oblivion right as that bitch, Alexa, tapped me on the shoulder. Perfect. Just perfect.

But he's so damn tall, and hot, and intense. And he smelled amazing. His hand on mine made me tingle, made me light-headed and giddy. Zach's attention made me feel like the most beautiful woman in the room.

Okay, so dancing with Zach had been spectacular. I didn't regret that part. And, if I'm being totally honest, I didn't regret the grinding, either. In fact, half the reason I was so miserable this weekend was because of just how badly I wanted to do it again.

Naked maybe. In my bed. Or the shower. Hell, the living room floor would do.

Yep. No maybe about that one, definitely naked.

But he asked Alexa to the party, not me. Of all people, that vile, wretched, horrible witch, whose life mission appears to be to make me miserable at work.

I had to admit the dirty truth. Alexa is hot, in a skanky kind of way. Her make-up is always perfect. I see her coming out of the gym down the street on a regular basis, every inch of her body toned and smooth and fucking perfect.

I hate her. Just a little. And I have no doubt that they left the party together, drove to her place and started fucking by the time I opened my second box of tissues. And now I would have to face both of them, together.

Unfortunately, I can't escape reality forever. The elevator doors open and I head down the aisle to my desk only to find her sitting at my desk going through my things. She looks gorgeous, of course. Her long blond hair is in an elaborate twist. Her black skirt is short, tight, and shows off legs that go on forever before they reach four-inch, strappy, cute-as-hell heels.

Resisting temptation is hard, but I don't glance down at my own black silk pants, dark blue blouse and comfortable, sling-back pumps. I'm wearing mascara and a bit of blush, but that's it. Per the usual.

Alexa looks like she just stepped out of a salon. And,

she got to fuck Zach this weekend. Kiss him. Rub her perfect body all over him.

Yep. I hate her.

"Alexa? What are you doing at my desk?"

"You're late." Alexa doesn't even look my way. She's sitting on the edge of my desk, rifling through my folders.

"I'm not late, this is the same time I get here every day." Not that she would know. She never arrives when she is supposed to, always at least an hour late. "What are you looking for?"

"We have a very important meeting this morning. We're presenting the rollout plan for the new model to the executive team."

My heart jumps in my chest. Finally! I've been working on that project for two months. "It's not on my desk. I didn't print anything out. It's all in the cloud."

Shrugging, she gets off my desk and sits her perfect ass in my chair like it belongs to her. She lifts a few manila folders, opens them, rifles through my files and puts them down. With a sigh, she looks me in the eye. "I need you in that meeting, Bethany."

"Okay. Great." Perhaps I shouldn't hate her. I've been waiting for this opportunity forever.

She pats me on the shoulder, but I ignore the urge to push her away from me. "I'll see you in there. But I need you to copy me on the marketing plan now so I can go over it before we go in."

I don't like that, but I can't say no. "All right."

Alexa stands up and waves me toward my chair, my

desk. With her heels on, she's taller than I am and I wish I'd worn better shoes. "Now would be good. The meeting starts in ten minutes."

In a panic I rush around the corner of my desk. "The presentation isn't ready. It'll take me at least thirty minutes to pull it together. Why didn't you tell me last week?"

Alexa crosses her arms. "I emailed you this weekend. If you had been doing your job, like you were supposed to, you would have known. If you don't pull your shit together everyone will see that you've dropped the ball. And what's with you? You look like shit. Are you sick?"

Well, then. I move firmly back into the it's-okay-to-hate-her camp. "I'm fine, now move so I can get this done."

Alexa stands way too close with her arms still folded. "If you screw this up for me and make me look bad, you're done." She steps aside and walks away before turning back to face me. "Oh, and don't think I didn't notice your little stunt at the Christmas party. You threw yourself at Zach and you knew he was there with me. I saw you grinding on him like a little bitch in heat. I mean, really Bethany? Did you even dream he would go for a little mouse like you? Real men, hard men, need a real woman who can keep up with them. And trust me, little mouse, that's not you, not even in your wildest dreams."

"Just go so I can do my job." I turn my back on her, sit down and log into my computer.

Alexa leans over my shoulder and whispers in my ear. "If you value your career, I suggest you stay far, far away from Zach. He's mine. Cross me on this, and you will never work in this field again. I'll make sure of it." She turns, walks into her office and slams the door.

I hate the bitch but at least I will get the chance to present my work to the executive team. I worked for two months on the marketing plan and I'm certain they will love it. To finally get to demonstrate my capabilities and my hard work is a dream come true. I've been dying for the opportunity to show them what I can do and move out from under Alexa's shadow.

Ten minutes? I glance at the clock on the wall. Now I've got eight. I rush through the final two slides as Alexa passes by my desk on her way to the conference room.

"Hi, Zach," Alexa calls and I see him out of the corner of my eye. For a moment I think he's headed my way, but she moves to intercept him. "Are you ready for the meeting? Let me show you the new brochure." I don't move as they pass by. I can't bring myself to look at him.

With an eye on the clock in the corner of my computer I finish the presentation and open my email to send it to Alexa. I'm pissed to discover that she emailed me about the meeting this weekend. Any other weekend, I would have seen the message and finished my work. But this time I laid around pissed off and licking my wounds. I have no doubt she knew I wouldn't check my work email, not after that party. Not after the *grinding incident*. Still, she could have thrown me a bone and followed the weekend email with a text. It's not like she didn't win in the end.

She got Zach.

I press send on the presentation and check the clock. They are only ten minutes into the meeting and I hope they are just getting started.

I jump up and rush to the conference room. As I open the door and enter the back of the room, I see Alexa speaking to the group with Jack Simpson, the CEO, at the head of the table. Zach is seated to his right.

"Is there something we can do for you, Bethany?" Alexa calls from the front of the room. She's walking in front of the projector screen, my newly emailed presentation in bright lights.

"You told me you wanted me in this meeting."

"Yes, sweetie. Thank you. We need you to get the coffee order." Her smile is pure honey as she waves toward the counter on the other side of the room. "The order is on a piece of paper in the back. Thank you so much. And please, hurry back. We all need some caffeine."

Frozen as much by Zach's dark stare as I am by her fake smile, I can't figure out what to do. "I thought... I was going to present the roll-out plan."

"Oh no, sweetie. I can present my own marketing plan. This meeting is for the executive team. Now can you hurry? We have some thirsty men in here."

I'm mortified. Did she ask me to come to this meeting just so she could degrade me, send me for coffee and take credit for my hard work? I'm speechless and stunned as everyone stares. My hand trembles as I reach for the coffee order but stop inches from the piece of yellow legal paper.

I've got a dozen pair of eyes glued to my back wondering why I'm here. My shoulders are tense, fragile as glass and ready to shatter.

Fuck this. And fuck her.

I turn on my sling-back heels and cross my arms. "No. You're a fraud and a liar. I'm not doing it." What little focus had shifted away from me roars back and every face in the room is looking my direction. I don't care. "That is *my* marketing plan, Alexa, and you know it."

"Please honey, you're embarrassing yourself." She waves me off as if I'm an annoying fly trying to land on her arm.

"Are you seriously going to stand there and try to take credit for *my* work, when you continually do nothing day after day?" This job is a lost cause at this point. And I will not be this bitch's doormat. And Zach? He's hot, but he can go fuck himself, too.

"Now that's enough, Bethany. You are on treading on thin ice." Alexa wags her finger in my direction.

"Jack, sir…" I say before Alexa interrupts.

"That's it." Alexa moves between the CEO and me. "Bethany, you're done, leave, now."

"Are you firing me?" I am nearing tears but don't want to humiliate myself any further so I hold back.

"You've done it to yourself."

"Bethany, wait." Zach stands behind Alexa and I can no longer contain myself.

"No, you know what? It's fine Zach. You deserve each other. And I don't have to put up with this. I'm out of here." I turn and storm out the door not bothering to stop at my desk and clear out my things.

8

I NEED MY BEST FRIEND. I need Lindsey.

I haven't heard from her since I left for the Christmas party and she didn't respond to any of my texts over the weekend so I head for the coffee shop. It's Monday morning so there is a high probability I will find her there. Then I can bitch at her for not returning my texts. She better have a damn good reason, like being tied up to her boss's bed all weekend.

I'm so angry that I make the trip to the Get Perky coffee shop in half the normal time. I open the doors and am greeted by the familiar aroma of brewing coffee grounds and acoustic guitar music floating in the air. My mood brightens, if only just slightly, but Lindsey is not here. *Screw it*, I need coffee anyway so I get in the queue.

"Well hello dearie." I hear a voice I recognize speak from behind me in line and I turn.

"Oh, hello again," I say to the old woman with the magical touch and she is smiling at me again.

"It's almost Christmas. Do you think you'll get all that you wished for?"

"It doesn't seem so." Then it occurs to me she might remember Lindsey from last week. "You haven't seen the woman I sat with last time, have you?"

"No, I'm sorry I haven't. I could use some company though. Would you like to sit with me?"

"Sure, why not?"

As we sit and talk, I find her delightful, grace personified. Her outfit is perfect, accessorized with matching jewelry and handbag. Her hair looks as though she just left the salon and her makeup is flawless. She rushes nothing, savoring every sip of coffee and each morsel of her pasty. And she listens, attentive to every detail as I pour my heart out. She doesn't judge me or offer solutions. She listens. Before I realize two hours have passed, the lunch crowd files in and Lindsey walks through the door.

"Lindsey." I wave to her. She waves back and gets in line.

"Well, dearie, I'll be on my way now. I'm sure you'll be wanting to talk to your friend." The grey-haired woman stands and gathers her black leather gloves. Before she puts them on she grabs my hand and I recognize the familiar magical sensation. "Listen to me Beth," she says. "Don't give up on love. I promise you won't be disappointed. Old ladies understand things and this old lady knows more than most." She winks and puts on her gloves as she walks to the door. "Trust me and have faith, magic is in the air this holiday season."

"Wait." I call to her. "I never got your name."

"I'm Opal." She smiles. "We'll meet again." She turns and pauses as an elderly man opens the door for her and she is gone.

"Who was that?" Lindsey asks as she approaches the table.

"Where have you been?" I stand up and scowl at her. "Let's go, you're taking me to your place. We have a lot to talk about."

"What's going on?" Coffee in hand, she follows me out the door and rushes to my side. "I take it things didn't go well at the party."

"Umm, you could say that. And I think I just got fired… or I quit, I'm not really sure which."

"What happened? Beth, what did you do?"

"It was the supreme bitch."

"Ah damn. Alexa? What'd she do?"

On the way to her apartment I tell her everything, well almost everything, I save the dance for the apartment. By the time we arrive at her door I'm freezing and my feet are killing me from walking the whole distance in my work shoes. I sit down, kick off my heels, start up the fireplace and wait as Lindsey makes hot chocolate.

"Marshmallows?" She yells from the kitchen.

"Whip Cream?" I yell back.

"Marshmallows."

"Sounds great." I say as she appears with a steaming cup overflowing with tiny colored marshmallows.

"Here you go." She hands me the cup and sits in the chair across from me. Somehow, she makes wearing a skirt and heels appear comfortable. And pantyhose. Hers have cute little black ribbon designs in them. They decorate her legs like a Christmas party all their own. God, I freaking hate pantyhose.

Legs tucked beneath her, Lindsey settles back in her seat. "Okay, now tell me everything and don't skip any details."

So, I talk. She sits in silence, nodding occasionally, absorbing everything and sipping at her cup. And then I get to the part where I grind on his erection on the dance floor, she jolts forward and spills cocoa on her adorable little ribbons. She's rubbing it away with her bare hand as she talks. "Wait, you guys were that close? No wonder Alexa freaked out."

"Yep."

"And how was it?" Cocoa emergency handled, she returns her full attention to me.

I tease, "How was what?"

"Bitch, don't hold back, you know what."

"Magnificent." I can't help but smile like a Cheshire cat.

"Tell me everything. I want the juicy details." She stands up and starts to pace.

I shouldn't mess with her like this, but I can't resist… "I thought I might come."

She whirls, her eyes sparkling. "And did you?"

"No, but I wanted to." I take the last sip of my hot chocolate and set my cup on the end table. "Instead, he left with that bitch and probably fucked her. She probably came more than once. Hell, she was probably coming all night long." I could just imagine her in bed with Zach. Snuggled up after sex, all sweaty and hot and reaching for his…

"Are you sure he spent the night with her?"

"No, but it's all I could think about the whole weekend as I sat around and pouted."

She crinkled up her nose. "You imagined them having sex?"

"I couldn't help hit."

"Ewwww, how could you?"

"Because he's smoking hot and I hate to admit it, but Alexa is attractive. So, really, it wasn't so bad." I pause, glance up at her and grin. "I thought I might come."

Lindsey screams and high-steps around the living room shaking her arms like she has the heebee jeebees, and then stops. "And did you?"

"No… but I wanted to." We both burst into laughter and she jumps into my chair. She hugs me and I forget all about my stupid job. If only forgetting about Zach Steal was that easy.

Zach

IT'S BEEN three days since she ran out of the meeting and I haven't seen her since. She never even came back to the office to clean out her desk. Not that there was much there. I checked her desk. Lip gloss. A nail file. Typical female stuff.

But there was nothing personal there. No photos or anything. Nothing for her to come back for.

Me included, I guess. Bethany told me, loud and clear, what she thought of me and Alexa in that conference room.

Thinking about her rage made me equal parts ashamed and horny as fuck. She was hot when she was mad, her green eyes spitting fire and her chest heaving.

I wanted that. I wanted *her*. So here I am, again, sitting in my truck outside her apartment building, a little bit like a stalker. But I am getting seriously worried. Nobody knows where she is.

Alexa treated Bethany horribly and I can't even imagine what she thinks of me. And so I wait. Again. At the very least, I need to apologize. And I don't care if it is Christmas Eve, she's got to come back, eventually.

I've got nowhere better to be, so I'll sit here and wait. I turn up the fan on my heater and lean back into the seat of my truck to get comfortable. Now I know what cops go through on a stakeout.

It's almost ten o'clock and I shake my head to keep myself awake. I reach for my coffee and she appears from around the corner of the building. Her chin is tucked down as she heads for the front door. Adrenaline shoots straight to my heart, I jump out of my truck, wave and yell. "Bethany."

She looks at me, squinting through those sexy fucking glasses, but doesn't stop walking. So I run.

I don't know the code to her building, and I don't trust her to buzz me through, so I scramble to grab the door and sigh in relief when I catch it.

It's warmer inside, but not by much. The cold, industrial tile on the floor is meant to handle a lot of traffic, not look pretty. I stomp the snow off my boots and wonder if she picked up her pace when she entered the building. She's disappearing inside an elevator. I run, but by the time I reach her, I have to jam my arm between the closing elevator doors.

The annoying buzz of the elevator alarm fills the quiet and I wince, but the doors open and there she is. Her blond hair is wild and loose around her shoulders and her face is fresh and bare of make-up. Her lips are pink and full and all I want to do is get that heavy coat off her body, unwrap her like my very own Christmas present.

"What do you want, Zach?" She won't even look me

in the eyes. But she's staring at my lips, so all hope is not lost.

I am out of breath from running after her in the cold. At least that's what I tell myself. I'm thirty-four years old. I don't get nervous around women. "Where have you been?"

She raises her brow when I step onto the elevator, then shrugs and pushes the button for the third floor. "Why do you care?"

"I've been looking for you for three days." She turns to face me, her eyes wide with surprise and her jaw drops. Adorable. Flustered and fucking perfect. Suddenly, every hour spent sitting in my truck like a psycho stalker seems worth it.

"Why? Do you have my final paycheck or an invitation to your wedding with Alexa? Or some other way you'd like to ruin my life?"

Okay. So, not so flustered, but cute as hell. She's pissed. And after the way Alexa treated her, I can't blame her.

"How did I ruin your life?" I ask, as we step out onto the third floor and I follow her to her door. "I don't even like Alexa."

She has her key in the lock, refusing to look at me. I think I'm screwed, but she pauses before she turns the key. "Could have fooled me. Didn't you have an "appointment" with her after your last dance? Didn't you go back to her place?" She mimic's Alexa's cloying tone, and puts her hand on my arm, batting her eyelashes up at me almost exactly like Alexa did. I don't like it. "'*Zach*, honey, *just one more dance and we can head back to my place.*'"

"I didn't leave with her."

"You came with her."

Damn it. "You were engaged, Bethany. You had a huge diamond ring on your finger, remember?"

That seems to take some of the air out of her sails. Thank God, because I'm not going to let her put me in a box or tell me I did anything wrong. I wanted her, and if she'd stuck around long enough for me to tell her, we'd be inside this apartment right now. She'd already be naked and wet and ready. "I chased after you, but you are exceptionally fast in high heels."

"You did?"

"Yes. I did. I saw you jump in that guy's car, but he tore out of there before I could stop you." I place my hand on her shoulder and turn her to face me. She doesn't resist my touch, which I take as a hopeful sign. "Who was that guy anyway?"

"The cab driver?"

"That wasn't a taxi. Bethany, the car wasn't even yellow."

"It wasn't?" She looks into my eyes and tears are streaming down her face.

"No." I reach up with my hand and stop a tear from reaching her chin.

"You were chasing me?"

I nod and reach down to grab her hands with mine.

She shakes her head and gets a sheepish grin on her

face. "No wonder he didn't charge me for the ride." She giggles and sniffles. "But why, Zach?"

"Why what?"

"Why were you chasing me? And why are you here? Aren't you with Alexa?"

"I want to finish what we started on that dance floor. I can't stop thinking about you." I am relieved to see that the tears have stopped. "And I don't like Alexa at all, she is not a very nice person. I have been here for three days straight, waiting for you to come back. I thought maybe you fled the country, and I'd have to chase you to Brazil or something."

"You'd do that?"

"You bet your beautiful ass I would."

"You'd extradite me?"

"Yep." I pull her in for a hug and squeeze hard, content when she melts against me. She's fluffy in her coat, but I don't care. She's in my arms, exactly where I want her.

"And you think I have a beautiful ass?"

"Oh yeah." It's all I can do to fight off the urge to grab it.

"Zachary Steal?" She whispers in my ear.

"Yes, Bethany Riley?"

She pulls back and looks me in the eye. "Would you like to come inside?"

9

I SMILE as she pulls me into her apartment. "Oh, hell yes."

The door closes behind us and I reach for both her hands again as she drops her keys where she stands. They crash to the floor but neither one of us cares. I spin with her and shove her up against the door, raise her arms above her head as our fingers intertwine and my mouth is on hers. We kiss and I can't get enough. I'm drowning, like time itself came to a halt so I could savor the taste of her. My cock swells to full in an instant.

I press hard against her body to signal my intentions. If I could fuck her right then and right there without releasing her hands I would. But there's too much stuff in the way. I can't hold her here *and* get her naked.

She whimpers through her tongue as she shoves it deeper to meet mine and presses her hips hard against me. For a moment I wish for a clone so the second version of me could strip her bare while the first me holds her in this kiss and never lets go of her hands.

No such luck. I pull back, though I don't let go of her hands, and I find myself panting as I gaze up and down her entire body. Her coat fell open and my head spins at the sight of a tight yellow blouse with buttons straining to contain her ample breasts. Her nipples are clearly visible through the thin fabric. Bare. "Don't move your hands."

"Okay." She's breathless as I release my hold on her hands and lower my fingers to the center of her shirt, my knuckles scrape the soft inner swells of her breasts. I grasp the thin fabric, hot as fuck when I see her eyes dark with desire. She holds my gaze, her hands still lifted and held against the door above her head.

She's mine. She's so fucking mine.

"Do you care about this shirt?" I ask as I peer into her eyes.

"No. It's not mine, it's Lindsey's."

"Lindsey must be…umm…smaller than you." She grins as I tear the two sides of the blouse apart. Buttons explode from the fabric, rattle across the hardwood floor in every direction.

I am treated to a most spectacular vision. Two of the

most magnificent breasts I have ever seen heave out and down, unrestrained. Her nipples are a dark rose, erect and hardening in the cool air of the apartment. My aggression rocked them and I watch, almost hypnotized, as they settle in perfect alignment, begging for my attention.

Both of her hands are still above her head and I grasp them in my right hand as I reach behind her waist with my left to pull her hips toward mine. I lower my head to her left breast and suck her hardened nipple into my mouth. She arches her back, her hands tugging to be free. But I hold her still, unwilling to release her as she tilts her head back and moans.

The divine taste of her skin is like a drug to my senses and I'm instantly addicted. My cock strains to break free, to burst from its confines and ravage her body, but I pull back and stare at the ground to contain myself. And I breathe. This moment is too perfect to rush; I have too many things I need to do to this woman.

So I plot.

"Where is your bedroom?"

I let go of her hands and she brushes her breasts across my body as she heads to the back of the apartment. She strolls, I follow. I reach to her shoulders to pull what remains of the ripped blouse down her arms and free from her body. She never stops moving while she kicks off her shoes and I expose her pale skin to the night. Goose bumps rise on her flesh.

As we enter her bedroom she pauses, removes her

glasses, places them on her dresser and turns to face me.

"Uh-uh." I reach for her glasses. "These are the same glasses you had on at the party, right?"

"Yes." She nods. "I'm sorry they didn't match my dress. I wanted them to be red."

"No, I love these glasses." I place them back on her face. "Leave them on."

I look down to see her beautiful breasts; nipples hardened and erect. The skin of her stomach is smooth and supple and I trail my fingertips over her chilled flesh to the top of her jeans.

I release each button one by one and kneel to pull her pants and a pink pair of lace panties down each leg. She lifts her legs, each one in turn and I pull the jeans free from her body. I place my hands behind her, each palm spread over a side of her tight, round ass and pull her toward me while I place my nose just above her shaved pussy. I inhale deeply to absorb her scent, her wet aroma, and I know she is ready. She runs her hand through the back of my hair and moans. "Zach, please."

I stand and gaze into her eyes. "Oh no." I say. "Don't rush me. I've dreamt of this moment for a long time."

I turn my head to the right and notice a white gold necklace on her dresser. I grab the necklace and hand it to her before I step back to remove my shirt and watch. "Put this on."

She works the clasp, separating the two sides as I wait. With a twist of her neck she flicks her long blonde hair over her shoulders and raises her hands behind her neck. Her exquisite breasts raise and separate with the motion of her arms. After she has affixed the necklace, she drops her slender arms to the side of her curved and hourglass shape, her heavy breasts sway back into position and she awaits my inspection.

I drink in the picture of her, follow the length of her arms down to her delicate hands and I remember. The ring. Is it gone? I can't go any further until I know. "What happened to your engagement ring?"

"I gave it back, it's over. It was barely an engagement anyway. We didn't love each other." She steps forward and reaches for me. "And I didn't want him."

"What do you want?"

"I want you, Zach."

"You're sure about that. The way I feel right now, the thoughts that are going through my head, you sure you're ready for that?" I can barely contain myself so I pace side to side, never taking my eyes from her sensual body. "I like to have my way in the bedroom, you'll have to obey me. Can you handle what I will do to you?"

"Will you discipline me if I don't?" She pouts like a tease and I can barely breathe as I watch her hand trace a line from her lips to her cleavage. "What if I'm naughty?"

Oh my God. I can't believe this woman. Is she real or did I fall asleep in my truck and imagine this whole thing? "I'll spank that sweet ass," I answer.

"Promises, promises, Zach. You're not the only one who's dreamt of this moment." Her eyes smile seductively and she raises her left eyebrow in blatant challenge.

Moonlight shines through her windows and reflects off the silver sheen of the necklace, illuminating her pale, perfect skin. She is naked from head to toe but for the shining necklace and those fucking glasses.

She is the very vision of perfection. I am staring at a goddess, a goddess that wants to be tamed.

Time to make her mine.

1 0

ethany

As I STAND naked before him I can't believe the words that are coming out of my mouth. His chiseled face is half shadow, the moonlight doesn't show me his eyes but I can see that he's totally, completely, utterly focused on me. He's looking at me like no man ever has and I'm drunk with feminine power. Instead of hiding my body, I tilt my hips and thrust my breasts out to push him. I want him crazy. I want him to lose his fucking mind.

What has gotten into you, Bethany?

I scold myself for all of five seconds before naughty me answers.

Into me? Zach. As quickly as possible.

Into. As in, inside. Deep and hard and every daydream I ever had come to life.

He is so damn hot as he paces before me like a caged tiger. With every turn his chest flexes and his abs twist, his breath is heavy. He wants me as much as I want him. I can sense his desire from across the room and I'm so wet I can't believe my juices aren't running down my leg.

If he wanted to, he could bend me over my bed and take me right now, I'm that ready. And I'd let him.

I will let him do whatever he wants.

He steps forward at last and I lower my head, looking at the floor as I brace myself for what I hope is about to happen. He places his hand beneath my chin and raises my eyes to meet his. "Look at me." His voice is deep and sultry. And I do.

"Turn around," he commands.

And I do that, too.

As I turn away from him his hand settles at the center of my back, pushing me until I crawl onto the bed.

He moves his hand up to my shoulder and holds me tight. "Stop. Did I tell you to get on the bed?"

"No."

"Then don't. Now bend over."

I bend over my bed with my feet still on the floor and my legs straight as I glance back at him over my shoulder. I can't believe what I am about to say, but I can't help myself. Every dark fantasy I've ever had is spinning inside my head and I know—somehow I know—Zach will give me whatever I want, no matter how dirty.

"I'm sorry I was bad, Zach. Are you going to spank me?"

Smack. His swift hand shakes my entire ass and my flesh burns. I shudder with anticipation as I bury my face in my bed to muffle the cry that erupts from my throat. He's a shadow behind me, dark and demanding and so hot I can't think, I can only need.

I want more.

"If you don't do as I tell you, you will get worse."

He moves both of his hands to my round ass and massages each side. My entire core is stretched and exposed to the air, and to his will. He continues to massage the left side while his right hand slides deep down the center and the side of his hand brushes across my anus. Elliott never neared my backside, and I am surprised at the sensation. But Zach doesn't linger. His fingers pass and he slides his index finger into my wetness.

I am delirious. My entire being is focused on the finger fucking me. My wetness coats his finger, and he slides in and out, slow at first, then faster. He doesn't rush, but I want him to. I would stay in this position all day and just let him do this to me but, apparently, he has other ideas.

He adds a second finger, his large digits stretching me wide. God it's good. So good. But I want more.

I want him.

He thrusts inside, then out, his third and fourth

fingers massage my clit and I groan into the bed. Every thrust of his hand drives his palm into me.

I'm going to come all over his hand. I'm close. So close.

But I need him to fuck me harder. I need more. I push back against his hand and try to ride him the way I want it.

Smack, smack.

Fire. My ass is on fire and I love it.

"I didn't tell you to move." He pulls his right hand from me at the first trembling warnings of an orgasm.

"Zach, no please." I beg. I'm on the edge. He can't leave me like this.

"Turn over."

The command fills me with heat and I roll over onto my back. My bottom is on the edge of the bed, my feet on the floor. Zach grabs an ankle in each hand. He places a foot on each of his muscular shoulders as he bends down to suck my clit into his mouth. He sucks in and out as he presses his tongue over my nub and plunges his two fingers back in my pussy. Within seconds I am nearing my peak again. He pushes harder and faster, flicking my clit with the tip of his tongue and I am there.

I fall apart, his name on my lips as I lose control, my insides throb and spasm on his hand.

He watches me come. I open my eyes to see his gaze locked onto my face.

"You're fucking beautiful when you come." He rises from between my legs like a conqueror and all I can think about is getting his cock inside me. Now. Right now.

I close my eyes, but Zach's having none of it. And he's not done with me yet.

"Look at me." I open my eyes to see his muscular chest and shoulders. I trace every line, every detail. I could stare at him for hours. His tattoos are elaborate and stretch over most of his torso in a complex design it will take me hours to explore with my lips. If he'll let me, I'll trace every single line of ink.

He hovers over me, his fingers gently rubbing my clit like he owns that one special spot, as if it belongs to him. "Get on your knees and take off my pants."

I slide off the bed, sink to the floor and open his zipper. As I pull apart the two sides and slide his clothing over his tight ass, I catch my first sight of his massive cock. It springs free of his pants and I'm not sure I can wrap my hand around the thick length.

Oh my. He pressed against me on the dance floor, but I had no idea that it would be so thick, easily twice as thick as poor Elliott.

His pants reach the floor and he steps out of them, grabs the back of my hair and tilts my head back. "Open your mouth."

"I've never…." I start to tell him I've never had oral sex. It's not that I didn't want to, but Elliott was never interested.

"Don't make me bend you over my knee," he interrupts. "Open your mouth."

I open my mouth as wide as I can. He grabs his cock

with his other hand and slides it in my mouth. I've never tasted a man before. I thought I would hate it, but I don't. I'm intoxicated by his musky flavor, by the way he moans when I suck him down, by the shudder in his thighs when I run my tongue around the tip.

He holds my head, slides his cock in and out of my mouth as I clamp down with my lips and press my eager tongue along the bottom of his huge cock.

"Slow down." He pulls his cock from my mouth and helps me to my feet. "I want to cum inside you, but not there, not this time."

I want that, too. I want to own every bit of him the way I suspect he's about to own me.

"LIE DOWN ON THE BED, on your stomach." Zach's voice is a whisper, but I sear every word is like a drum beat inside my body.

I do as he commands and I wait for him to join me. He stands over me and I gaze back at him in question.

"You are amazing." His eyes wander up and down the back of my body.

I smile and turn my face into the bed to wait. Seems Zach likes to take his time and look his fill. I'm okay with that, as long as he's looking at me.

A moment later he joins me on the bed. He spreads my legs and kneels between them before he reaches for my wrists and completes my spread eagle pose. And then he covers my body with his. The pressure of his hard body presses me into the bed. The weight is delicious and heady and I'm completely under his control. His hot lips nuzzle and kiss the back of my neck. His cock slides between the mounds of my ass and down to my core as he continues to cover my neck and back with gentle kisses. He slides up and down, rubbing his cock against me over and over, but never where I want him. Inside.

"God, Zach. Are you trying to kill me? Fuck me. Do it."

I become so aroused by the pressure of his body, the slide of his cock on my ass and the passion of his kisses that I can't resist lifting my hips in blatant invitation.

He pulls back and I think I will get what I want, finally!

Smack, smack, smack!

Stinging heat spreads through me. He reddens my ass harder and faster this time but it only makes me crazier, more desperate, as every nerve ending in my body is on fire. "Have you already forgotten? I didn't tell you to move."

With the sting of his hand ringing through my body, all the way to my clit, I groan into the bed. I never knew how excited I could be by a man that commands me in bed, disciplines me to his desire.

He grabs the side of my hip, flips me over and pulls me so my feet are at the base of the bed. I'm on my back and he kneels above me, his hips just above my head. He looks down at me before he covers me. We're full on sixty-nine now and he lowers his mouth to my shaved mound.

His muscles flex as he holds his weight off me with one hand. With the other, he slides two fingers along my wet folds, all the way down to the sides of my ass. I'm distracted as the wetness from my pussy has spread to my ass, chilled now in the cold air. His cock is hanging in front of me. All I have to do is turn my head, just a little, and he'll be mine.

He pinches my clit and massages it between his fingers.

"Now take my cock in your mouth," he orders. "But don't make me cum."

I do as he says but cannot concentrate on the task he has given me. He doesn't seem to notice because he is thrusting his fingers in and out of my pussy and moving hard and fast on my clit. I moan with his cock in my throat as he pushes me to come again. I lose it when he sucks my clit into his mouth and flicks it with his tongue. My core clamps down on his fingers like a fist and I'm bucking and out of control.

I release his cock from my mouth and glance up to find him watching me. Again. I have never had this much attention from a man, not one that could do what Zach does with such ease and command. And I've never been happier. "You will ruin me." I rub my hand up and down the inside of his muscular thigh.

"We're not done yet."

I smile. We're not done yet. "Please tell me you have a condom?"

He rises and walks to his discarded pants. I watch him, enjoying the view of his wide shoulders and tight ass. In seconds he's back, his huge cock covered and ready when he crawls down the bed and kneels between my thighs. He pushes my knees wide and uses my hips to pull me close. I'm spread before him and all I can focus on is his cock. I want his cock inside; I need him inside me, filling me.

He places the massive head at my core and rocks forward with a groan. I tilt my neck back as the pressure rises and close my eyes to wait. He grabs his base with his hand and slides along my folds to moisten the head of his cock. I nearly jump out of my skin every time he brushes across my sensitized nub before he moves down and presses deep inside me with one, smooth thrust.

I am stretched and open, vulnerable as I've never been before. He continues to drive deep inside again and again, arching his back while he drives his hips forward filling me completely. With every thrust his balls press against my bottom. He drives into me faster and faster like a piston and I'm ready to scream, the orgasm coming for me like a tidal wave to crush me.

He's buried balls deep when he stops, holding us locked together and denying me release yet again.

"Zach!"

He chuckles and I straighten my glasses to see him.

"I love those sexy, schoolteacher glasses."

I reach for him. I want him covering me. I want his

skin on mine. I want his weight pressing me into the bed. I want to feel like I belong to him.

He gives me what I want, lowering himself on top of me, his cock buried deep. He kisses me fully, thrusting slow, but hard, rocking over me. Into me.

I kiss him back with everything but he pulls away.

"Open your eyes." He commands, and I do.

With his full body weight on me, his belly grinds on my clit while his cock works back and forth. We stare into each other's eyes, and he drives faster and harder until he swells inside me. He's going to come, and the knowledge pushes me over again. Gaze locked to his, my insides clamp down on his cock again and again as he moans a guttural groan and releases his seed deep inside me.

When it's over, he collapses on top of me. He's still inside me, and that's exactly where I want him. We lay there fighting for air for an eternity as I run my fingers up and down his back.

After long minutes, I need more air. He senses my body tensing and rolls to his back. I am bereft for less than a second before he pulls my head to rest on his shoulder. I'm tucked against his side like I belong there, his arms are around me and our legs are entwined. I take my opportunity and trace a beautiful line of ink with my fingertip from his shoulder to his neck.

As I lay there listening to his heartbeat, I notice the clock has passed twelve o'clock. "Merry Christmas." I rub my hand across his chest. He doesn't respond right away and I am not sure if he's still awake. I stop moving and he lifts his hand to mine, grabs my wrist and mimics my movements. "Don't stop."

"I thought you were asleep."

"No." He opens his eyes. "You were distracting me. Is it Christmas already?"

"Yep."

"Merry Christmas to you, too." He kisses my forehead.

"I didn't get you a gift." I tease.

"I think you just gave me my gift." He smiles and closes his eyes.

"I guess you're nicer than I am."

"Why do you say that?"

"You gave me three."

He chuckles, but it's buried in a yawn. "I am pretty damn nice." Zach pulls the covers out from under us and tucks us in, somehow keeping me plastered to his side. Before I know it, he is breathing the deep breath of sleep and I follow soon after.

ach

MY EYES open and it takes a moment for them to focus. It takes longer for me to recognize where I am.

Bethany isn't in bed, but I can hear she hasn't gone far. I hear dishes clinking in the kitchen and the aroma of fresh brewed coffee has reached the bedroom. I roll over to check the time. Ten o'clock. Wow, ten hours of sleep. I haven't had ten hours of uninterrupted sleep in ages. The pitter-patter of bare feet heads my way, and she walks into the room. Naked but for the glasses and necklace. And she's carrying two steaming cups of coffee.

I sit up and stuff a pillow behind my back. "I don't think I have ever seen anything so perfect in my life."

"You want coffee?" She stands in the doorway and

shifts her hips from left to right, grinning from ear to ear. I crook my finger at her and she comes. I could get used to this real fucking quick.

"Are you trying to make me fall in love with you already?" I reach out and take a cup from her as she sits beside me on the bed.

"That's all it takes? Coffee?" She grins and rolls her eyes as she takes a sip from her own cup. "I must have missed that memo."

"What can I say? I'm easy." I sip from my cup and it's just the way I like it, hot, dark and black. God, this woman is perfect. "Merry Christmas, by the way. At least we don't have to go to work today."

"Are you forgetting? I don't have a job anymore." She pauses and looks away. "But you're right, and I'm broke. I'll have to start looking for a new job tomorrow."

"Why don't you just take Alexa's?" She doesn't understand and I grin as I sip my coffee, waiting for her to figure it out.

"What are you talking about?" Bethany lowers her forgotten coffee to the bedside table and stares at me like I've grown two heads. "Did she quit?"

"Nah. I fired her. Did you think I would let her get away with treating you like that?" Bethany was mine, and I protected what belonged to me. It was time she understood the score. Now that I'd tasted her, I wasn't letting her go.

Her green eyes were wide with confusion and I

wanted to pump my fist into the air in triumph. Fuck yeah.

"What do you mean you fired her? How could you fire her? What did Jack say?"

"Jack didn't have any say. Not that he was sad to see her go." I sip my coffee again, slowly, drawing out the moment. Bethany naked, her long blond hair not quite covering her bare breasts. Those glasses. Those lips. Even the little crease between her eyebrows as she tries to figure me out is adorable.

"What do you mean? He's the CEO."

"Jack's my boy. I'm the one who hired him to be CEO."

"I don't get it."

If I wasn't in love with her before, I fell hard and fast with those four words. I put my cup down next to hers on the bedside table and lift both hands to frame her beautiful, clueless face.

"You really don't know, do you?" I trace her full lower lip with my thumb, barely able to resist the urge to kiss her.

"Know what?"

"Know that I own a large stake of the company."

She shakes her head, so I continue. "They brought me in when they started the company. All the founders were tech guys."

"I'm aware of that. Big money out of Silicon Valley."

"Right. They wanted to design cool electric bikes, but they didn't have much experience with real motorcycles. That's where I come in. I bring the cool factor, make sure the bikes are beautiful and perform great."

"You know bikes?" Bethany was watching me, listening, but her tongue flicked over the end of my thumb and I strained to focus, to remember what I was telling her. I wanted her to understand I was more than just a bad boy. Hell, I was trying to impress her and she was not responding the way most women did.

"They needed me to make the whole thing work, so the bikes would appeal to regular motorcycle types, so I demanded twenty percent equity."

"Twenty percent?" I pause and watch, delighted, as the wheels start to spin. "Twenty percent of a company worth…"

"Yep." Feeling a little sheepish, I shrug. "Who knew the company would be so successful?"

"That means you're a…"

"Yep."

"With a b?"

"Yep. A *capital* B."

"Holy Cow." She jumps up, full of energy, and paces the room. "I can't believe it. I just thought you were the super-hot biker guy that worked in the shop."

"Well, I am." I smile and cross my arms. "Super-hot."

"With a *capital* S?" Her eyes flash as her gaze meets mine, but she's smiling. Bethany didn't care if I was a simple shop guy. She doesn't give a shit that I'm rich as fucking Midas either. And I couldn't take my eyes off her. Every step and her breasts sway, her hips swing side to side in a feminine prowl.

"You better stop parading around like that, or I might just get some bad ideas."

She puts a knee on the end of the bed and crawls toward me on all fours. Her breasts hang beneath her, pure temptation. "That sounds okay to me. We have all day."

"I'll need to shower, eventually. Does this place have a shower?"

"Oh, we can shower all right." A wicked grin spreads across her face.

"And what does that mean?"

"Oh, nothing." She raises her left eyebrow and moves closer. "We could also go to your place and shower. Your place is probably nicer than mine."

"A little bit. It's a bachelor's pad, though. Not a cozy pillow, fringe lampshade or fluffy, flowered duvet in sight."

She pauses before she asks, "Do you have a king size bed?"

"Yes."

"Do you have an arm chair at the end of that bed?"

"Yes."

"Hmmm." She smiles.

"Why?"

"I'd like to see that." I have no idea what she is talking about. But I like it.

 ethany

ZACH and I stopped by the office this morning so he could drop off a sketch for his new design. I told him it could probably wait. It's New Year's Eve and nobody is really working today anyway. They're all home getting ready for the big party. But he insisted, and I agreed on one condition; we stop for coffee at Get Perky.

It's not like I had to twist his arm. Since we started dating, Get Perky has become his favorite coffee shop too. In fact, he goes there more than I do now.

As we near the front entrance, I can't wait to get inside and get warm. The damp cold this time of year just has a way of seeping into my bones. I can't get warm unless I'm naked and snuggled up with Zach.

Doesn't matter how cold I am. He makes me hot in two-point-five kisses.

Zach steps ahead of me to open the door and stands aside so I can enter. He is such a gentleman. Who knew? He may appear to be a bad boy and, in bed, he is. But in every other way he is a perfect gentleman. Sometimes I pinch myself to make sure that I'm not daydreaming again. He's almost too good to be real. If it weren't for the delicious soreness between my legs, I might question my sanity.

I follow him to the front counter but notice Lindsey sitting at a corner table. And she's not alone. I can't help but smile when I see who is keeping her company. It's Opal. She's wearing a bright red jumper today. Her short hair is curled perfectly and her lips, as usual, are a bright, brilliant red.

"Can you order me a vanilla latte?" I tug on Zach's sleeve. "I'm going to go say hi. Lindsey's here."

"Sure, for a kiss."

Oh, the agony. I pull his head down to mine in front of everyone and lay one on him because I can. Because he's mine now and I like to remind him of that fact. And because he's so fucking hot I can't resist.

Heart pounding, I release Zach and turn toward Lindsey's table. I see Opal getting up to leave, but she has Lindsey's hand in hers.

"Hey, Opal." My smile is a mile wide and I don't hold back. If I didn't think it would freak her out, I'd grab the elderly woman in a full-on bear hug. Without her, I wouldn't have had the confidence to pour my body into that little red dress and go for Zach.

"Oh, hello, dear." She's holding a pair of gloves again, but they're red this time, not black.

"New gloves?"

"Oh no, I have a matching pair for every outfit." She reaches over and grabs my hand. Her touch is warm this time; like hot cocoa, a cozy fireplace and a good book all in one. "I saw you with that kiss. Everything turned out just wonderful, didn't it?"

"Better than wonderful." Zach must have placed our order because he is walking our way. Every time I see him, my heart aches and I can't believe he's mine. "Opal, I want you to meet someone."

Before I have a chance to introduce them, Opal reaches out and grabs Zach's hand. "Well hello, Zach." I search my memory, trying to recall if I ever mentioned his name. I'm pretty darn sure that I had not.

"Hello." He looks down at her hand and smiles at her touch.

"Have you two met?" I ask Zach, but Opal interrupts.

"You two make such a lovely couple." She releases our hands and begins to put on her gloves. "I couldn't be happier for you. You'll be very happy together." Then she turns and smiles at Lindsey. "Honey, I enjoyed our conversation so much. Remember what I said. We'll meet again."

Zach and I turn to watch as she walks to the door.

An elderly gentleman opens the door and holds it for her. She passes through the door and disappears.

"Who was that?" Zach asks.

Lindsey stands up, looks to the door and answers. "That's Opal, she's delightful."

I turn to Lindsey "That's exactly what I said after I met her, delightful."

Zach is staring at the door with a wistful expression on his face. "She was delightful, wasn't she?"

I almost burst out laughing. I doubt those words have ever come out of his mouth before. Opal has that effect on people.

Coffee shop Chris has come out from behind the counter to give us our coffee. "Here's your coffee, Zach."

"Thanks, Chris." Zach takes two cups from him and hands one to me.

"What the hell is this?" Lindsey grabs my hand, nearly spilling my coffee before I can switch the cup to my right hand. "What is this rock quarry on your finger? You bitch, you didn't? Why didn't you tell me?"

"It just happened this morning. We haven't had a chance to tell anyone yet." And that was the truth. I'd barely processed it myself. Zach, on one knee, promising to love me forever. That wasn't exactly an everyday occurrence. I was still floating on a cloud. My entire body tingled every time I looked at him. It was all there in his gaze. Love. Lust. Utter devotion. Everything I'd always wanted and never thought I'd actually get.

Every person in the coffee shop turns to stare as

Lindsey screams and grabs Zach in a giant hug. She shakes him so hard his coffee sloshes over the edges of his cup and onto the floor.

"Welcome to the family big guy." She reaches out an arm and yanks me into their embrace. "We're going to be so happy." She rocks us so hard I spill my coffee, too.

Chris looks at the floor and sighs, "I guess I'm going to have to clean that up." He shakes his head at Lindsey and turns away. "I knew you two were going to be so much trouble."

Zach pulls me close until I'm nestled under his shoulder, exactly where I want to be. Lindsey looks at the mess on the floor then back up at me. We smile at each other and yell in unison. "Sorry, Chris."

I hope you enjoyed Bethany and Zach's whirlwind romance! Find out what matchmaking mischief the delightful Opal has up her sleeve in the next Magical Matchmaker book... **Billionaire's Obsession!**

Michael: I have three rules I live by when building multi-billion-dollar companies. Rule one: don't sleep with employees. Rule two: never, ever, ever sleep with your employees. Rule three: listen idiot, you can't have her!

Only now… she quit… and the rules no longer apply. Getting her to say yes won't be easy... I think she enjoys watching me sweat.

ABOUT THE AUTHOR

JOIN Amanda's VIP Reader List!
http://bit.ly/AmandaNews

Amanda Adams writes funny, sexy, new adult and contemporary romance, as well as a new YA romantic cozy mystery series. A full time author, Amanda spends her days trying to walk more and type less. If she eats a salad for lunch, she makes sure to reward herself with chocolate after (as any reasonable woman would do.) Her books are free of cheating--with a guaranteed HEA. Enjoy!

Connect with Amanda:
Facebook: http://bit.ly/AmandaAFacebook
Twitter: @amandaadamsauth
www.amandaadamsauthor.com

9 781795 901031